Poetry
by Heart

**To Helen
and Nicholas**

First published in the United Kingdom in 2001 by The Chicken House,
2 Palmer Street, Frome, Somerset BA11 1DS.

Book design by Mandy Sherliker

Library of Congress Cataloging-in-Publication Data available

ISBN 0-439-29657-9

10 9 8 7 6 5 4 3 2 1   01 02 03 04 05

Printed in Italy

First American edition, September 2001

Poetry by Heart

A Child's Book of Poems to Remember

FOREWORD BY ANDREW MOTION

COMPILED BY LIZ ATTENBOROUGH

The Chicken House
SCHOLASTIC INC
New York

CONTENTS

FOREWORD

"Learning by heart" has a bad reputation. Most of us adults have memories of dim and distant school-rooms, in which we see ourselves half-crouched, half-slumped over a desk, alternately nibbling our fingers and mumbling as we try and cram into our heads some lines of poetry we don't entirely understand and certainly don't like. But really that isn't a memory of "learning by heart". It's a memory of "learning by rote," dull, vaguely frightening and dry as a dog biscuit.

The difference between "heart" and "rote" is important. If we say we know something "by heart," we mean we keep it in our closest and most inward and important place, because it matters so much to us. It is a way of showing love, and of preserving it. And since poetry is something which deals with the most important things in our life – with pleasure, dread, excitement, love itself – it seems entirely right and proper that we should have it "by heart" as well.

And poetry makes it easy to do this. As we grow up, we learn more and more subtle languages to describe how words work, how they make us feel, what they contain. But we never lose (or we never should lose) our sense of words as very primitive things, and of poems as primitive things too. Little children take to chanting, to making sound-patterns, as readily as they do to licking chocolatey spoons – and they remember these chants without any effort or resentment. All too often, of course, this essential pleasure in poetry, this feeling that it appeals to something fundamental in our human natures, is damaged as we grow up. We don't have time. Or we have a boring teacher. Whatever. But the fact is: poetry is always there, waiting for us to come back to it. Of course poetry can be difficult. Of course it can be demanding. But it is also something which exists in us as surely as we exist in it.

The poems gathered in this book prove what I mean. It's full of chants of one kind or another – the so-called nonsense of "Eenie, meenie, mackeracka," or William Blake's thrilling "Tyger, Tyger," or the skipping lyrics of more recent poets like Charles Causley and John Agard. However clever the poems are – and some of them are very clever – they have that element of the primitive.

And what about the poems which are not so obviously chants? Are they more difficult to take to heart? I don't think so. After all, poems affect us in all kinds of different ways – with their violin music as well as their drum music, with their formal patterns of rhyme, with their pictures. These are all primitive pleasures too – and as we enjoy them, we realize that the way we understand a poem is only partly to do with what the words mean as they lie on the page. It has just as much to do with the sounds they make, and the associations they strike up.

So enjoy the book! That's what it's here for: enjoyment, as well as edification. By taking the poems to heart now, you'll be saving something that will stay with you all your lives, changing and growing as you change and grow.

Andrew Motion, 2001

INTRODUCTION

As you flick through this book you will come across poems that you know, or that spark a memory in you. I hope you will also find some new poems that you haven't seen before, but would like to know better.

The book starts with a section of very short poems, quick and easy to learn by heart and recite again whenever the mood comes. The other sections are loosely grouped together under themes, and they only represent a tiny selection of all the many different poems that would have been suitable to add to this book.

But this book also has something extra to help with your learning – a brilliant array of illustrations that will add to your visual images of the words, which will be a powerful tool to help you remember. Read the words, see the pictures, create a vivid scene. As you re-read and remember you will vary the way you say certain phrases until it all sounds just right, and maybe even find yourself flinging your arms about. The poems you remember best will be the ones that mean something special or conjure a particular picture or memory for you, so start with one of those. Then move to others which seem particularly interesting or moving or funny.

It is tedious to learn words just one after another, as if you were doing a spelling test. If you come across words or phrases that cause difficulties, use your own pictures in your head to help you remember. Link those pictures to the words before and the words that come after, and before long you have a kind of photograph in your head of how it all fits together. Some lines will practically lend themselves to be sung, such is the strength of their rhythm and sound pattern.

Some of the poems you learn will stay with you forever, for your mind to recall throughout your life. They might come to mind when you are in a beautiful place, or going through a sad time, or when you see something funny. The clever poets in this book have used words in a way that captures their thoughts and dreams, and sometimes when you read them you think they might have been written just for you. By putting them in your memory, they can become yours.

This book will be just the start for you, as there is a wealth of poetry published to read and enjoy. Why not make your own book of poems that feel just so special that you want to have them in your head and your heart for always?

Liz Attenborough, 2001

Short *and*
Sharp

Singing-Time

I wake in the morning early
And always, the very first thing,
I poke out my head and I sit up in bed
And I sing and I sing and I sing.

Rose Fyleman

Three Little Owls Who Sang Hymns

There were three little owls in a wood
Who sang hymns whenever they could;
What the words were about
One could never make out,
But one felt it was doing them good.

Anonymous

Bengal

There once was a man of Bengal
Who was asked to a fancy dress ball;
He murmured: 'I'll risk it
and go as a biscuit…'
But a dog ate him up in the hall.

Anonymous

Three Grey Geese

Three grey geese in a green field grazing
Grey were the geese and green was the grazing.

Anonymous

Whole Duty of Children

A child should always say what's true,
And speak when he is spoken to,
And behave mannerly at table:
At least as far as he is able.

Robert Louis Stevenson

I Eat My Peas With Honey

I eat my peas with honey,
I've done it all my life:
It makes the peas taste funny,
But it keeps them on the knife.

Anonymous

There Was an Old Person of Wilts

There was an Old Person of Wilts,
Who constantly walked upon stilts;
He wreathed them with lilies, and daffydown-dillies,
That elegant person of Wilts.

Edward Lear

Said the General

Said the General of the Army,
'I think that war is barmy'
So he threw away his gun:
Now he's having much more fun.
Spike Milligan

It's Hard to Lose Your Lover

It's hard to lose your lover
When your heart is full of hope
But it's worse to lose your towel
When your eyes are full of soap.
Anonymous

Boy   Girl
Boy   Girl
Garden   Gate
Standing   Kissing
Very   Late
Dad   Comes
Big   Boots
Boy   Runs
Girl   Scoots

Anonymous

Four Seasons

Spring is showery, flowery, bowery.
Summer: hoppy, choppy, poppy.
Autumn: wheezy, sneezy, freezy.
Winter: slippy, drippy, nippy.

Anonymous

Whether the Weather

Whether the weather be fine
Or whether the weather be not
Whether the weather be cold
Or whether the weather be hot –
We'll weather the weather
Whatever the weather
Whether we like it or not!

Anonymous

Starlight

Starlight, star bright,
First star I see tonight,
I wish I may, I wish I might,
Have the wish I wish tonight.

Anonymous

Little wind

Little wind, blow on the hill-top,
Little wind, blow down the plain;
Little wind, blow up the sunshine,
Little wind, blow off the rain.

Kate Greenaway

21

Ecka, Decka, Donie, Creka

Ecka, decka, donie, creka,
Ecka, decka, do;
Ease, cheese, butter, bread,
Out goes you.

Anonymous

Chinese Counting

Eenie, meenie, mackeracka,
Hi, di, dominacka,
Stickeracka, roomeracka,
Om, pom, push.

Anonymous

Thumping, Stumping, Bumping, Jumping

Thumping, stumping, bumping, jumping,
Ripping, nipping, tripping, skipping,
All the way home.

Popping, clopping, stopping, hopping,
Stalking, chalking, talking, walking,
All the way home.
Anonymous

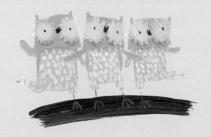

Squeezes

We love to squeeze bananas,
We love to squeeze ripe plums,
And when they are feeling sad
We love to squeeze our mums.

Brian Patten

Fur *and* Feathers

The Frog

Be kind and tender to the Frog,
    And do not call him names,
As 'Slimy skin,' or 'Polly-wog,'
    Or likewise 'Ugly James,'
Or 'Gape-a-grin,' or 'Toad-gone-wrong,'
    Or 'Billy Bandy-knees':
The Frog is justly sensitive
    To epithets like these.
No animal will more repay
    A treatment kind and fair;
At least so lonely people say
Who keep a frog (and, by the way,
    They are extremely rare).

Hilaire Belloc

Ducks' Ditty

All along the backwater,
Through the rushes tall,
Ducks are a-dabbling,
Up tails all!

Ducks' tails, drakes' tails,
Yellow feet a-quiver,
Yellow bills all out of sight
Busy in the river!

Slushy green undergrowth
Where the roach swim –
Here we keep our larder
Cool and full and dim.

Every one for what he likes!
We like to be
Heads down, tails up,
Dabbling free!

High in the blue above
Swifts whirl and call –
We are down a-dabbling,
Up tails all!
                    Kenneth Grahame

from
The Swallow

Pretty swallow, once again
Come and pass me in the rain.
Pretty swallow, why so shy?
Pass again my window by.

Pretty little swallow, fly
Village doors and windows by,
Whisking o'er the garden pales
Where the blackbird finds the snails;

On yon low-thatched cottage stop,
In the sooty chimney pop,
Where thy wife and family
Every evening wait for thee.

John Clare

A Fly and a Flea

A fly and a flea in a flue
Were imprisoned, so what could they do?
 Said the fly, 'let us flee!'
 'Let us fly!' said the flea.
So they flew through a flaw in the flue.

Anonymous

Sing, Said the Mother

Over in the meadows in the nest in
   the tree
Lived an old mother birdy and her
   little birdies three.
Sing, said the mother. We sing,
   said the three.
So they sang and were glad in the nest
   in the tree.

Over in the meadows in the sand in the sun
Lived an old mother toady and her
   little toady one.
Hop, said the mother. We hop, said the one.
So they hopped and were glad in the sand
   in the sun.

Over in the meadows in a sly little den
Lived an old mother spider and her
   little spiders ten.
Spin, said the mother. We spin, said the ten.
So they spun and caught flies in their
   sly little den.

Anonymous

I Had a Little Cat

I had a little cat called Tim Tom Tay,
I took him to town on market day,
I combed his whiskers, I brushed his tail,
I wrote on a label, 'Cat for Sale.
Knows how to deal with rats and mice.
Two pounds fifty. Bargain price.'

But when the people came to buy
I saw such a look in Tim Tom's eye
That it was clear as clear could be
I couldn't sell Tim for a fortune's fee.
I was shamed and sorry, I'll tell you plain,
And I took home Tim Tom Tay again.

Charles Causley

Walking the Dog Seems Like Fun to Me

I said, The dog wants a walk.

Mum said to Dad, It's your turn.
Dad said, I always walk the dog.
Mum said, Well I walked her this morning.
Dad said, She's your dog.
I didn't want a dog in the first place.

Mum said, It's your turn.

Dad stood up and threw the remote control
at the pot plant.
Dad said, I'm going down the pub.
Mum said, Take the dog.

Dad shouted, No way!
Mum shouted, You're going nowhere!

I grabbed Judy's lead
and we both bolted out the back door.

The stars were shining like diamonds.
Judy sniffed at a hedgehog, rolled up in a ball.
She ate a discarded kebab on the pavement.
She tried to chase a cat that ran up a tree.

Walking the dog
seems like fun to me.

Roger Stevens

The Goldfish

Through the ice swept clear of snow
There suddenly appeared a glow,

A glow of orange, then a glower,
A gaping, vacant-featured flower,

A flower which floated up, a face
Against the limits of its space,

Its space I gazed at vacantly,
As distant as eternity,

Eternity, unnumbered years
Of thought which comes then disappears,

Then disappears, a guilty wish,
As quickly as that flowery fish,

That flowery fish which turned about,
Flickered, dimmed and then went out,

Went out like a fading light
Into the darkness, far from sight,

From sight, but never far from mind,
Leaving its after-glow behind,

Behind, before, just once, not twice,
No second glances through the ice.

John Mole

Something Told the Wild Geese

Something told the wild geese
   It was time to go.
Though the field lay golden
   Something whispered, 'Snow.'
Leaves were green and stirring,
   Berries, lustre-glossed,
But beneath warm feathers
   Something cautioned, 'Frost.'
All the sagging orchards
   Steamed with amber spice,
But each wild breast stiffened
   At remembered ice.
Something told the wild geese
   It was time to fly –
Summer sun was on their wings,
   Winter in their cry.

Rachel Field

33

The Tyger

Tyger, tyger burning bright
In the forests of the night,
What immortal hand or eye
Could frame thy fearful symmetry?

In what distant deeps or skies
Burnt the fire of thine eyes?
On what wings dare he aspire?
What the hand dare seize the fire?

And what shoulder and what art
Could twist the sinews of thy heart?
And, when thy heart began to beat,
What dread hand and what dread feet?

What the hammer? What the chain?
In what furnace was thy brain?
What the anvil? What dread grasp
Dare its deadly terrors clasp?

When the stars threw down their spears,
And water'd heaven with their tears,
Did He smile His work to see?
Did He who made the lamb make thee?

Tyger, tyger, burning bright
In the forests of the night,
What immortal hand or eye
Dare frame thy fearful symmetry?

William Blake

Dogs

I had a little dog,
    and my dog was very small.
He licked me in the face,
    and he answered to my call.
Of all the treasures that were mine,
    I loved him best of all.

Frances Cornford

Stuff *and* Nonsense

Miss Polly Had a Dolly

Miss Polly had a dolly who was sick, sick, sick,
So she phoned for the doctor to be quick, quick, quick.
The doctor came with his bag and his hat,
And he knocked on the door with a rat-a-tat-tat.

He looked at the dolly and he shook his head,
And he said, 'Miss Polly, put her straight to bed.'
He wrote on a paper for a pill, pill, pill,
'I'll be back in the morning with my bill, bill, bill.'

Anonymous

Betty Botter

Betty Botter bought some butter,
But, she said, this butter's bitter;
If I put it in my batter,
It will make my batter bitter,
But a bit of better butter
Will make my batter better.
So she bought a bit of butter
Better than her bitter butter,
And she put it in her batter,
And it made her batter better,
So 'twas better Betty Botter
Bought a bit of better butter.

Anonymous

Yellow Butter

Yellow butter purple jelly red jam black bread

Spread it thick
Say it quick

Yellow butter purple jelly red jam black bread

Spread it thicker
Say it quicker

Yellow butter purple jelly red jam black bread

Now repeat it
While you eat it

Yellow butter purple jelly red jam black bread

Don't talk
With your mouth full!

Mary Ann Hoberman

39

I Saw a Jolly Hunter

I saw a jolly hunter
  With a jolly gun
Walking in the country
  In the jolly sun.

In the jolly meadow
  Sat a jolly hare.
Saw the jolly hunter.
  Took jolly care.

Hunter jolly eager –
  Sight of jolly prey.
Forgot gun pointing
  Wrong jolly way.

Jolly hunter jolly head
  Over heels gone.
Jolly old safety catch
  Not jolly on.

Bang went the jolly gun.
  Hunter jolly dead.
Jolly hare got clean away.
  Jolly good, I said.

Charles Causley

There Was an Old Man

There was an Old Man, who when little
Fell casually into a kettle;
But, growing too stout, he could never get out,
So he passed all his life in that kettle.

Edward Lear

Noise

Billy is blowing his trumpet;
Bertie is banging a tin;
Betty is crying for mummy
And Bob has pricked Ben with a pin.
Baby is crying out loudly;
He's out on the lawn in his pram.
I am the only one silent
And I've eaten all of the jam.

Anonymous

Alphabet Stew

Words can be stuffy, as sticky as glue,
but words can be tutored to tickle you too,
to rumble and tumble and tingle and sing,
to buzz like a bumblebee, coil like a spring.

Juggle their letters and jumble their sounds,
swirl them in circles and stack them in mounds,
twist them and tease them and turn them about,
teach them to dance upside down, inside out.

Make mighty words whisper and tiny words roar
in ways no one ever had thought of before;
cook an improbable alphabet stew,
and words will reveal little secrets to you.

Jack Prelutsky

Look Out!

The witches mumble horrid chants,
You're scolded by five thousand aunts,
  A Martian pulls a fearsome face
  And hurls you into Outer Space,
You're tied in front of whistling trains,
A tomahawk has sliced your brains,
  The tigers snarl, the giants roar,
  You're sat on by a dinosaur.
In vain you're shouting 'Help' and 'Stop',
The walls are spinning like a top,
  The earth is melting in the sun
  And all the horror's just begun.
And, oh, the screams, the thumping hearts
That awful night before school starts.

Max Fatchen

The Owl and the Pussy-Cat

The Owl and the Pussy-Cat went to sea
  In a beautiful pea-green boat,
They took some honey, and plenty of money,
  Wrapped up in a five-pound note.
The Owl looked up to the stars above,
  And sang to a small guitar,
'O lovely Pussy! O Pussy, my love,
  What a beautiful Pussy you are,
    You are,
    You are!
  What a beautiful Pussy you are!'

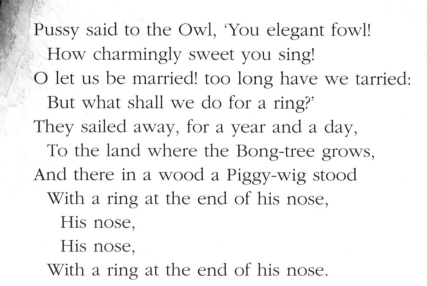

Pussy said to the Owl, 'You elegant fowl!
  How charmingly sweet you sing!
O let us be married! too long have we tarried:
  But what shall we do for a ring?'
They sailed away, for a year and a day,
  To the land where the Bong-tree grows,
And there in a wood a Piggy-wig stood
  With a ring at the end of his nose,
    His nose,
    His nose,
  With a ring at the end of his nose.

'Dear Pig, are you willing to sell for one shilling
   Your ring?' Said the Piggy, 'I will.'
So they took it away, and were married next day
   By the Turkey who lives on the hill.
They dined on mince, and slices of quince,
Which they ate with a runcible spoon;
And hand in hand, on the edge of the sand,
   They danced by the light of the moon,
      The moon,
      The moon,
   They danced by the light of the moon.

                              Edward Lear

How Doth the Little Crocodile

How doth the little crocodile
  Improve his shining tail,
And pour the waters of the Nile
  On every golden scale!

How cheerfully he seems to grin,
  How neatly spreads his claws,
And welcomes little fishes in
  With gently smiling jaws!

Lewis Carroll

Jumper

When I was a lad as big as my Dad,
I jumped into a pea-pod;
Pea-pod was so full,
I jumped into a roaring bull;
Roaring bull was so fat,
I jumped into a gentleman's hat;
Gentleman's hat was so fine,
I jumped into a bottle of wine;
Bottle of wine was so clear,
I jumped into a bottle of beer;
Bottle of beer was so thick,
I jumped into a knobbed stick;
Knobbed stick wouldn't bend,
I jumped into a turkey hen;
Turkey hen wouldn't lay,
I jumped into a piece of clay;
Piece of clay was so nasty,
I jumped into an apple pasty;
Apple pasty was so good,
I jumped into a lump of wood;
Lump of wood was so rotten,
I jumped into a bale of cotton;
The bale of cotton set on fire,
Blew me up to Jeremiah;
Jeremiah was a prophet,
Had a horse and couldn't stop it;
Horse knocked against t'ould cobbler's door,
Knocked t'ould cobbler on the floor;
Cobbler with his rusty gun,
Shot the horse and off it run.

Anonymous

W

The King sent for his Wise Men all
  To find a rhyme for W;
When they had thought a good long time
But could not think of a single rhyme,
  'I'm sorry,' said he, 'to trouble you.'

James Reeves

Uplifting
and Brave

When a Knight Won his Spurs

When a knight won his spurs, in the stories of old,
He was gentle and brave, he was gallant and bold;
With a shield on his arm and a lance in his hand
For God and for valour he rode through the land.

No charger have I, and no sword by my side,
Yet still to adventure and battle I ride,
Though back into storyland giants have fled,
And the knights are no more and the dragons are dead.

Let faith be my shield and let joy be my steed
'Gainst the dragons of anger, the ogres of greed;
And let me set free, with the sword of my youth,
From the castle of darkness the power of the truth.

Jan Struther

Heroes

Heroes are funny people, dey are lost an found
Sum heroes are brainy an sum are muscle-bound,
Plenty heroes die poor an are heroes after dying
Sum heroes mek yu smile when yu feel like crying.
Sum heroes are made heroes as a political trick
Sum heroes are sensible an sum are very thick!
Sum heroes are not heroes cause dey do not play de game
A hero can be young or old and have a silly name.
Drunks an sober types alike hav heroes of dere kind
Most heroes are heroes out of sight an out of mind,
Sum heroes shine a light upon a place where darkness fell
Yu could be a hero soon, yes, yu can never tell.
So if yu see a hero, better treat dem wid respect
Poets an painters say heroes are a prime subject,
Most people hav heroes even though some don't admit
I say we're all heroes if we do our little bit.

Benjamin Zephaniah

Lone Dog

I'm a lean dog, a keen dog, a wild dog and lone,
I'm a rough dog, a tough dog, hunting on my own!
I'm a bad dog, a mad dog, teasing silly sheep;
I love to sit and bay the moon and keep fat souls from sleep.

I'll never be a lap dog, licking dirty feet,
A sleek dog, a meek dog, cringing for my meat.
Not for me the fireside, the well-filled plate,
But shut door and sharp stone and cuff and kick and hate.

Not for me the other dogs, running by my side,
Some have run a short while, but none of them would bide.
O mine is still the lone trail, the hard trail, the best,
Wide wind and wild stars and the hunger of the quest.

Irene McLeod

The Eagle

He clasps the crag with crooked hands;
Close to the sun in lonely lands,
Ringed with the azure world, he stands.

The wrinkled sea beneath him crawls;
He watches from his mountain walls,
And like a thunderbolt he falls.

Alfred, Lord Tennyson

And My Heart Soars

The beauty of the trees,
the softness of the air,
the fragrance of the grass,
  speaks to me.

The summit of the mountain,
the thunder of the sky,
the rhythm of the sea,
  speaks to me.

The faintness of the stars,
the freshness of the morning,
the dew drop on the flower,
  speaks to me.

The strength of fire,
the taste of salmon,
the trail of the sun,
And the life that never goes away,
  They speak to me.

And my heart soars.

Chief Dan George

Everyone Sang

Everyone suddenly burst out singing;
And I was filled with such delight
As prisoned birds must find in freedom,
Winging wildly across the white
Orchards and dark-green fields; on – on – and out of sight.

Everyone's voice was suddenly lifted;
And beauty came like the setting sun:
My heart was shaken with tears; and horror
Drifted away... O, but Everyone
Was a bird; and the song was wordless; the singing will never
      be done.

Siegfried Sassoon

Sea Fever

I must go down to the seas again, to the lonely sea and
the sky,
And all I ask is a tall ship and a star to steer her by,
And the wheel's kick and the wind's song and the white
sail's shaking,
And a grey mist on the sea's face, and a grey dawn
breaking.

I must go down to the seas again, for the call of the
running tide
Is a wild call and a clear call that may not be denied;
And all I ask is a windy day with the white clouds flying,
And the flung spray and the blown spume, and the sea-
gulls crying.

I must go down to the seas again, to the vagrant gypsy
life,
To the gull's way and the whale's way where the wind's
like a whetted knife;
And all I ask is a merry yarn from a laughing fellow-
rover,
And quiet sleep and a sweet dream when the long trick's
over.

John Masefield

People

Some people talk and talk
and never say a thing.
Some people look at you
and birds begin to sing.

Some people laugh and laugh
and yet you want to cry.
Some people touch your hand
and music fills the sky.

Charlotte Zolotow

Once more unto the breach

Once more unto the breach, dear friends, once more,
Or close the wall up with our English dead.
In peace there's nothing so becomes a man
As modest stillness and humility,
But when the blast of war blows in our ears,
Then imitate the action of the tiger.
Stiffen the sinews, conjure up the blood,
Disguise fair nature with hard-favoured rage.
Then lend the eye a terrible aspect,
Let it pry through the portage of the head
Like the brass cannon, let the brow o'erwhelm it
As fearfully as doth a galled rock
O'erhang and jutty his confounded base,
Swilled with the wild and wasteful ocean.
Now set the teeth and stretch the nostril wide,
Hold hard the breath, and bend up every spirit
To his full height. On, on, you noblest English,
Whose blood is fet from fathers of war-proof,
Fathers that like so many Alexanders
Have in these parts from morn till even fought,
And sheathed their swords for lack of argument.
Dishonour not your mothers; now attest
That those whom you called fathers did beget you.

William Shakespeare Henry V

The Soldier

If I should die, think only this of me:
  That there's some corner of a foreign field
That is for ever England. There shall be
  In that rich earth a richer dust concealed;
A dust whom England bore, shaped, made aware,
  Gave, once, her flowers to love, her ways to roam,
A body of England's, breathing English air,
  Washed by the rivers, blessed by suns of home.

And think, this heart, all evil shed away,
  A pulse in the eternal mind, no less
    Gives somewhere back the thoughts by England given;
Her sights and sounds; dreams happy as her day;
  And laughter, learnt of friends; and gentleness,
  In hearts at peace, under an English heaven.

Rupert Brooke

My Heart Leaps Up

My heart leaps up when I behold
    A rainbow in the sky;
So was it when my life began,
So is it now I am a man,
So be it when I shall grow old,
    Or let me die!
The Child is father of the Man;
And I could wish my days to be
Bound each to each by natural piety.

William Wordsworth

Ghostly
and Ghastly

Windy Nights

Whenever the moon and stars are set,
   Whenever the wind is high,
All night long in the dark and wet,
   A man goes riding by.
Late in the night when the fires are out,
Why does he gallop and gallop about?

Whenever the trees are crying aloud,
   And ships are tossed at sea,
By, on the highway, low and loud,
   By at the gallop goes he.
By at the gallop he goes, and then
By he comes back at the gallop again.

Robert Louis Stevenson

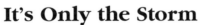

It's Only the Storm

'What's that creature that rattles the roof?'
'Hush, it's only the storm.'

'What's blowing the tiles and the branches off?'
'Hush, it's only the storm.'

'What's riding the sky like a wild white horse,
Flashing its teeth and stamping its hooves?'

'Hush, my dear, it's only the storm,
Racing the darkness till it catches the dawn.
Hush, my dear, it's only the storm,
When you wake in the morning, it will be gone.'

David Greygoose

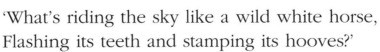

O What is That Sound

O what is that sound which so thrills the ear
   Down in the valley drumming, drumming?
Only the scarlet soldiers, dear,
   The soldiers coming.

O what is that light I see flashing so clear
   Over the distance brightly, brightly?
Only the sun on their weapons, dear,
   As they step lightly.

O what are they doing with all that gear,
   What are they doing this morning, this morning?
Only the usual manoeuvres, dear,
   Or perhaps a warning.

O why have they left the road down there,
   Why are they suddenly wheeling, wheeling?
Perhaps a change in the orders, dear.
   Why are you kneeling?

O haven't they stopped for the doctor's care,
   Haven't they reined their horses, their horses?
Why, they are none of them wounded, dear,
   None of these forces.

O is it the parson they want, with white hair,
  Is it the parson, is it, is it?
No, they are passing his gateway, dear,
  Without a visit.

O it must be the farmer who lives so near.
  It must be the farmer so cunning, so cunning?
They have passed the farmyard already, dear,
  And now they are running.

O where are you going? Stay with me here!
  Were the vows you swore deceiving, deceiving?
No, I promised to love you, dear,
  But I must be leaving.

O it's broken the lock and splintered the door,
  O it's the gate where they're turning, turning;
Their boots are heavy on the floor
  And their eyes are burning.

W. H. Auden

65

Duppy Dan

Duppy Dan
ain't no livin man

Duppy Dan
done dead an gone

Duppy Dan
nah have foot

Duppy Dan
nah have hand

Yet Duppy Dan cross water
Duppy Dan cross land

Duppy Dan ride white horse
pon pitch dark night

Run like-a-hell stranger
when Duppy Dan tell you goodnight

John Agard

Duppy is a Jamaican word for ghost

The Little Man

As I was walking up the stair
I met a man who wasn't there;
He wasn't there again today.
I wish, I wish he'd stay away.

Hughes Mearns

The Gentle Giant

Every night
At twelve o'clock,
The gentle giant
Takes a walk;
With a cry cried high
And a call called low,
The gentle giant
Walks below.

And as he walks,
He cries, he calls:

'Bad men, boogie men,
Bully men, shoo!
No one in the neighbour-
hood
Is scared of you.
The children are asleep,
And the parents are too:
Bad men, boogie men,
Bully men, shoo!'

Dennis Lee

Three Ghostesses

Three little ghostesses,
Sitting on postesses,
Eating buttered toastesses,
Greasing their fistesses,
Up to their wristesses,
Oh, what beastesses
To make such feastesses!

Anonymous

Extract from

George's Marvellous Medicine

So give me a bug and a jumping flea,
Give me two snails and lizards three,
And a slimy squiggler from the sea,
And the poisonous sting of a bumblebee,
And the juice from the fruit of the ju-jube tree,
And the powdered bone of a wombat's knee.
And one hundred other things as well
Each with a rather nasty smell.
I'll stir them up, I'll boil them long,
A mixture tough, a mixture strong.
And then, heigh-ho, and down it goes,
A nice big spoonful (hold your nose)
Just gulp it down and have no fear.
'How do you like it, Granny dear?'
Will she go pop? Will she explode?
Will she go flying down the road?
Will she go poof in a puff of smoke?
Start fizzing like a can of Coke?
Who knows? Not I. Let's wait and see.
(I'm glad it's neither you nor me.)
Oh Grandma, if you only knew
What I have got in store for you!

Roald Dahl

Round about the cauldron go

First Witch

Round about the cauldron go,
In the poisoned entrails throw.
Toad that under cold stone
Days and nights has thirty-one
Sweltered venom sleeping got,
Boil thou first i'th' charmed pot.

All

Double, double, toil and trouble,
Fire burn, and cauldron bubble.

William Shakespeare Macbeth

Waking Up

Oh! I have just had such a lovely dream!
And then I woke,
And all the dream went out like kettle-steam,
Or chimney-smoke.

My dream was all about – how funny, though!
I've only just
Dreamed it, and now it has begun to blow
Away like dust.

In it I went – no! in my dream I had –
No, that's not it!
I can't remember, oh, it is *too* bad,
My dream a bit.

But I saw something beautiful, I'm sure –
Then someone spoke,
And then I didn't see it any more,
Because I woke.

Eleanor Farjeon

Moonlit Apples

At the top of the house the apples are laid in rows,
And the skylight lets the moonlight in, and those
Apples are deep-sea apples of green. There goes
    A cloud on the moon in the autumn night.

A mouse in the wainscot scratches, and scratches, and then
There is no sound at the top of the house of men
Or mice; and the cloud is blown, and the moon again
    Dapples the apples with deep-sea light.

They are lying in rows there, under the gloomy beams;
On the sagging floor; they gather the silver streams
Out of the moon, those moonlit apples of dreams,
    And quiet is the steep stair under.

In the corridors under there is nothing but sleep.
And stiller than ever on orchard boughs they keep
Tryst with the moon, and deep is the silence, deep
    On the moon-washed apples of wonder.

John Drinkwater

Full Fathom Five

Full fathom five thy father lies,
    Of his bones are coral made;
Those are pearls that were his eyes;
    Nothing of him that doth fade,
But doth suffer a sea-change
Into something rich and strange.
Sea-nymphs hourly ring his knell:
    Ding-dong.
Hark! now I hear them – Ding-dong bell.
              William Shakespeare The Tempest

Love and Friendship

maggie and milly and molly and may

maggie and milly and molly and may
went down to the beach (to play one day)

and maggie discovered a shell that sang
so sweetly she couldn't remember
  her troubles, and

milly befriended a stranded star
whose rays five languid fingers were;

and molly was chased by a horrible thing
which raced sideways while blowing
  bubbles: and

may came home with a smooth round stone
so small as a world and as large as alone.

For whatever we lose (like a you or a me)
it's always ourselves we find in the sea.

e.e. cummings

Friends

I fear it's very wrong of me,
And yet I must admit.
When someone offers friendship
I want the *whole* of it.
I don't want everybody else
To share my friends with me.
At least, I want *one* special one,
Who, indisputably

Likes me much more than all the rest,
Who's always on my side,
Who never cares what others say,
Who lets me come and hide
Within his shadow, in his house –
It doesn't matter where –
Who lets me simply be myself,
Who's always, *always* there.
                    Elizabeth Jennings

my friend
my friend is
like bark
rounding a tree

he warms
like sun
on a winter day

he cools
like water
in the hot noon

his voice
is ready
as a spring bird

he is
my friend
and I
am his
Emily Hearn

My Shadow

I have a little shadow that goes in and out with me,
And what can be the use of him is more than I can see.
He is very, very like me from the heels up to the head;
And I see him jump before me, when I jump into my bed.

The funniest thing about him is the way he likes to grow –
Not at all like proper children, which is always very slow;
For he sometimes shoots up taller like an india-rubber ball,
And he sometimes gets so little that there's none of him at all.

He hasn't got a notion of how children ought to play,
And can only make a fool of me in every sort of way.
He stays so close beside me, he's a coward you can see;
I'd think shame to stick to nursie as that shadow sticks to me!

One morning, very early, before the sun was up,
I rose and found the shining dew on every buttercup;
But my lazy little shadow, like an arrant sleepy-head,
Had stayed at home behind me and was fast asleep in bed.

Robert Louis Stevenson

Lizzie Pitofsky Poem

I can't get enoughsky
Of Lizzie Pitofsky
I love her so much that it hurts.
I want her so terrible
I'd give her my gerbil
Plus twenty-two weeks of desserts.

I know that it's lovesky
'Cause Lizzie Pitofsky
Is turning me into a saint
I smell like a rose,
I've stopped picking my nose,
And I practically never say 'Ain't'.

I don't push and shovesky
'Cause Lizzie Pitofsky
Likes boys who are gentle and kind.
I'm not throwing rocks
And I'm changing my socks
(And to tell you the truth I don't mind)

Put tacks in my shoes,
Feed me vinegar juice,
And do other mean, bad, awful stuffsky.
But promise me this:
I won't die without kiss–
ing my glorious Lizzie Pitofsky.

Judith Viorst

First Love

When I was in my fourteenth year,
And captain of the third eleven,
I fell in love with Guenevere,
And hovered at the gate of heaven.
She wasn't more than twenty-seven.

I partnered her, by happy chance,
At tennis, losing every game.
No shadow dimmed her careless glance,
No teasing word, no hint of blame,
Brightlier burned my secret flame.

Nothing I asked but to adore,
In dumb surrender, shy and stiff:
But ah, she gave me how much more,
A benison beyond belief!
'Just hold my racquet for a jiff.'

Gerald Bullett

Valentine

My heart has made its mind up
And I'm afraid it's you.
Whatever you've got lined up,
My heart has made its mind up
And if you can't be signed up
This year, next year will do.
My heart has made its mind up
And I'm afraid it's you.

Wendy Cope

The Irreplaceable Mum

If you were a crack in the mirror,
If you were a flea on a cat,
If you were a slug in a jug,
I'd still love you, I wouldn't mind that.

If you were a smudge on a picture
Or an opera singer struck dumb,
If you were a pain in the neck then
You'd still be my very best chum.

If you were a fly in a pizza,
If you were a difficult sum,
Even if you were humpy and grumpy
You'd still be irreplaceable, Mum.

Brian Patten

Me

My Mum is on a diet,
My Dad is on the booze,
My Gran's out playing Bingo
And she was born to lose.

My brother's stripped his motorbike
Although it's bound to rain.
My sister's playing Elton John
Over and over again.

What a dim old family!
What a dreary lot!
Sometimes I think that I'm the only
Superstar they've got.

Kit Wright

Give Yourself a Hug

Give yourself a hug
when you feel unloved

Give yourself a hug
when people put on airs
to make you feel a bug

Give yourself a hug
when everyone seems to give you
a cold-shoulder shrug

Give yourself a hug –
a big big hug

And keep on singing,
'Only one in a million like me
Only one in a million-billion-thrillion-zillion
like me.'

Grace Nichols

When You Are Old

When you are old and grey and full of sleep,
And nodding by the fire, take down this book,
And slowly read, and dream of the soft look
Your eyes had once, and of their shadows deep;

How many loved your moments of glad grace,
And loved your beauty with love false or true,
But one man loved the pilgrim soul in you,
And loved the sorrows of your changing face;

And bending down beside the glowing bars,
Murmur, a little sadly, how Love fled
And paced upon the mountains overhead
And hid his face amid a crowd of stars.

W. B. Yeats

Night

The night has a thousand eyes,
        And the day but one;
Yet the light of the bright world dies
        With the dying sun.

The mind has a thousand eyes,
        And the heart but one;
Yet the light of a whole life dies,
        When love is done.
                    Francis William Bourdillon

Wistful *and* Thoughtful

The Road Not Taken

Two roads diverged in a yellow wood,
And sorry I could not travel both
And be one traveller, long I stood
And looked down one as far as I could
To where it bent in the undergrowth;

Then took the other, as just as fair,
And having perhaps the better claim,
Because it was grassy and wanted wear;
Though as for that the passing there
Had worn them really about the same,

And both that morning equally lay
In leaves no step had trodden black.
Oh, I kept the first for another day!
Yet knowing how way leads on to way,
I doubted if I should ever come back.

I shall be telling this with a sigh
Somewhere ages and ages hence:
Two roads diverged in a wood, and I —
I took the one less travelled by,
And that has made all the difference.

Robert Frost

Silverly
Silverly,
   Silverly,
Over the
   Trees
The moon drifts
   By on a
Runaway
   Breeze.

Dozily,
   Dozily,
Deep in her
   Bed,
A little girl
   Dreams with the
Moon in her
   Head.
      Dennis Lee

Sky in the Pie!

Waiter, there's a sky in my pie
Remove it at once if you please
You can keep your incredible sunsets
I ordered mincemeat and cheese

I can't stand nightingales singing
Or clouds all burnished with gold
The whispering breeze is disturbing the peas
And making my chips go all cold

I don't care if the chef is an artist
Whose canvases hang in the Tate
I want two veg. and puff pastry
Not the Universe heaped on my plate

OK I'll try just a spoonful
I suppose I've got nothing to lose
Mm… the colours quite tickle the palette
With a blend of delicate hues

The sun has a custardy flavour
And the clouds are as light as air
And the wind a chewier texture
(With a hint of cinnamon there?)

This sky is simply delicious
Why haven't I tried it before?
I can chew my way through to Eternity
And still have room left for more

Having acquired a taste for the Cosmos
I'll polish this sunset off soon
I can't wait to tuck into the night sky
Waiter! Please bring me the Moon!

                              Roger McGough

I Remember, I Remember

I remember, I remember,
    The house where I was born,
The little window where the sun
    Came peeping in at morn;
He never came a wink too soon,
    Nor brought too long a day,
But now, I often wish the night
    Had borne my breath away.

I remember, I remember,
    The roses, red and white;
The violets, and the lily-cups,
    Those flowers made of light!
The lilacs where the robin built,
    And where my brother set
The laburnum on his birthday –
    The tree is living yet!

I remember, I remember,
    Where I was used to swing;
And thought the air must rush as fresh
    To swallows on the wing:
My spirit flew in feathers then,
    That is so heavy now,
And summer pools could hardly cool
    The fever on my brow!

I remember, I remember,
    The fir trees dark and high;
I used to think their slender tops
    Were close against the sky:
It was a childish ignorance,
    But now 'tis little joy
To know I'm farther off from Heav'n
    Than when I was a boy.

Thomas Hood

Who?

Who is that child I see wandering, wandering
Down by the side of the quivering stream?
Why does he seem not to hear, though I call to him?
Where does he come from, and what is his name?

Why do I see him at sunrise and sunset
Taking, in old-fashioned clothes, the same track?
Why, when he walks, does he cast not a shadow
Though the sun rises and falls at his back?

Why does the dust lie so thick on the hedgerow
By the great field where a horse pulls the plough?
Why do I see only meadows, where houses
Stand in a line by the riverside now?

Why does he move like a wraith by the water,
Soft as the thistledown on the breeze blown?
When I draw near him so that I may hear him,
Why does he say that his name is my own?

Charles Causley

First Morning

I was there on that first morning of creation
when heaven and earth occupied one space
and no one had heard of the human race.

I was there on that first morning of creation
when a river rushed from the belly of an egg
and a mountain rose from a golden yolk.

I was there on that first morning of creation
when the waters parted like magic cloth
and the birds shook feathers at the first joke.

John Agard

Morning

Will there really be a morning?
    Is there such a thing as day?
Could I see it from the mountains
    If I were as tall as they?
Has it feet like water lilies?
    Has it feathers like a bird?
Is it brought from famous countries
    Of which I've never heard?
Oh, some scholar! Oh, some sailor!
    Oh, some wise man from the skies!
Please to tell a little pilgrim,
    Where the place called morning lies!

Emily Dickinson

The Railway Children

When we climbed the slopes of the cutting
We were eye-level with the white cups
Of the telegraph poles and the sizzling wires.

Like lovely freehand they curved for miles
East and miles west beyond us, sagging
Under their burden of swallows.

We were small and thought we knew nothing
Worth knowing. We thought words travelled the wires
In the shiny pouches of raindrops.

Each one seeded full with the light
Of the sky, the gleam of the lines, and ourselves
So infinitesimally scaled

We could stream through the eye of a needle.

Seamus Heaney

The Secret Place

There's a place I go, inside myself,
        Where nobody else can be,
And none of my friends can tell it's there –
        Nobody knows but me.

It's hard to explain the way it feels,
        Or even where I go.
It isn't a place in time or space,
        But once I'm there, *I know.*

It's tiny, it's shiny, it can't be seen,
        But it's big as the sky at night. . .
I try to explain and it hurts my brain,
        But once I'm there, it's *right.*

There's a place I know inside myself,
        And it's neither big nor small,
And whenever I go, it feels as though
        I never left at all.

Dennis Lee

There Isn't Time!

There isn't time, there isn't time
To do the things I want to do,
With all the mountain-tops to climb,
And all the woods to wander through,
And all the seas to sail upon,
And everywhere there is to go,
And all the people, every one
Who lives upon the earth to know.
There's only time, there's only time
To know a few, and do a few,
And then sit down and make a rhyme
About the rest I want to do.

Eleanor Farjeon

95

New Sights

I like to see a thing I know
Has not been seen before,
That's why I cut my apple through
To look into the core.

It's nice to think, though many an eye
Has seen the ruddy skin,
Mine is the very first to spy
The five brown pips within.

Anonymous

Peace *and* Quiet

There is a Time

There is a time for everything,
and a season for every activity under heaven:
a time to be born and a time to die,
a time to plant and a time to uproot,
a time to kill and a time to heal,
a time to tear down and a time to build,
a time to weep and a time to laugh,
a time to mourn and a time to dance,
a time to scatter stones and a time to gather them,
a time to embrace and a time to refrain,
a time to search and a time to give up,
a time to keep and a time to throw away,
a time to tear and a time to mend,
a time to be silent and a time to speak,
a time to love and a time to hate,
a time for war and a time for peace.

Ecclesiastes 3, v 1-8

Leisure

What is this life if, full of care,
We have no time to stand and stare?

No time to stand beneath the boughs
And stare as long as sheep or cows.

No time to see, when woods we pass,
Where squirrels hide their nuts in grass.

No time to see, in broad daylight,
Streams full of stars, like skies at night.

No time to turn at Beauty's glance,
And watch her feet, how they can dance.

No time to wait till her mouth can
Enrich that smile her eyes began.

A poor life this if, full of care,
We have no time to stand and stare.

William Henry Davies

The School in August

The cloakroom pegs are empty now,
And locked the classroom door,
The hollow desks are dimmed with dust,
And slow across the floor
A sunbeam creeps between the chairs
Till the sun shines no more.

Who did their hair before this glass?
Who scratched 'Elaine loves Jill'
One drowsy summer sewing-class
With scissors on the sill?
Who practised this piano
Whose notes are now so still?

Ah, notices are taken down,
And scorebooks stowed away,
And seniors grow tomorrow
From the juniors today,
And even swimming groups can fade,
Games mistresses turn grey.

Philip Larkin

The Little Dancers

Lonely, save for a few faint stars, the sky
Dreams; and lonely, below, the little street
Into its gloom retires, secluded and shy.
Scarcely the dumb roar enters this soft retreat:
And all is dark, save where come flooding rays
From a tavern-window; there, to the brisk measure
Of an organ that down in an alley merrily plays,
Two children, all alone and no one by,
Holding their tattered frocks, thro' an airy maze
Of motion lightly threaded with nimble feet
Dance sedately; face to face they gaze,
Their eyes shining, grave with a perfect pleasure.

Laurence Binyon

Silver

Slowly, silently, now the moon
Walks the night in her silver shoon;
This way, and that, she peers, and sees
Silver fruit upon silver trees;
One by one the casements catch
Her beams beneath the silvery thatch;
Couched in his kennel, like a log,
With paws of silver sleeps the dog;
From their shadowy cote the white breasts peep
Of doves in a silver-feathered sleep;
A harvest mouse goes scampering by,
With silver claws, and silver eye;
And moveless fish in the water gleam,
By silver reeds in a silver stream.

Walter de la Mare

This I know

The light of day
cannot stay.
The fading sun
will not come
to anybody's calling.

The cold moon light
Is clear and white.
She will not go,
this I know,
'til all the stars have fallen.
Anne Corkett

I know a bank

I know a bank where the wild thyme blows,
Where oxlips and the nodding violet grows,
Quite overcanopied with luscious woodbine,
With sweet musk-roses, and with eglantine.
There sleeps Titania sometime of the night,
Lulled in these flowers with dances and delight;
And there the snake throws her enamelled skin,
Weed wide enough to wrap a fairy in.
William Shakespeare   A Midsummer Night's Dream

103

I Have Lived and I Have Loved

I have lived and I have loved;
I have waked and I have slept;
I have sung and I have danced;
I have smiled and I have wept;
I have won and wasted treasure;
I have had my fill of pleasure;
And all these things were weariness,
And some of them were dreariness.
And all these things – but two things
Were emptiness and pain:
And Love – it was the best of them;
And Sleep – worth all the rest of them.

Anonymous

Dreams

Hold fast to dreams
For if dreams die
Life is a broken-winged bird
That cannot fly.

Hold fast to dreams
For when dreams go
Life is a barren field
Frozen with snow.

Langston Hughes

The Heavenly City

I sigh for the heavenly country,
Where the heavenly people pass,
And the sea is as quiet as a mirror
Of beautiful, beautiful glass.

I walk in the heavenly field,
With lilies and poppies bright,
I am dressed in a heavenly coat
Of polished white.

When I walk in the heavenly parkland
My feet on the pastures are bare,
Tall waves the grass, but no harmful
Creature is there.

At night I fly over the housetops,
And stand on the bright moony beams;
Gold are all heaven's rivers,
And silver her streams.

Stevie Smith

He Wishes for the Cloths of Heaven

Had I the heavens' embroidered cloths,
Enwrought with golden and silver light,
The blue and the dim and the dark cloths
Of night and light and the half-light,
I would spread the cloths under your feet:
But I, being poor, have only my dreams;
I have spread my dreams under your feet;
Tread softly because you tread on my dreams.

W. B. Yeats

Happy the Man

Happy the man, and happy he alone,
    He who can call today his own:
    He who, secure within, can say,
Tomorrow do thy worst, for I have lived today.
    Be fair or foul or rain or shine
The joys I have possessed, in spite of fate, are mine.
Not Heaven itself upon the past has power,
But what has been, has been, and I have had my hour.

John Dryden

Long *and* Lingering

The Quangle Wangle's Hat

On the top of the Crumpetty Tree
   The Quangle Wangle sat,
But his face you could not see,
On account of his Beaver Hat.
For his Hat was a hundred and two feet wide,
With ribbons and bibbons on every side
And bells, and buttons, and loops, and lace,
So that nobody ever could see the face
   Of the Quangle Wangle Quee.

The Quangle Wangle said
   To himself on the Crumpetty Tree:
'Jam; and jelly; and bread;
Are the best of food for me!
But the longer I live on this Crumpetty Tree,
The plainer than ever it seems to me
That very few people come this way,
And that life on the whole is far from gay!'
   Said the Quangle Wangle Quee.

But there came to the Crumpetty Tree,
   Mr and Mrs Canary;
And they said: 'Did you ever see
   Any spot so charmingly airy?
May we build a nest on your lovely Hat?
Mr Quangle Wangle, grant us that!
O please let us come and build a nest
Of whatever material suits you best,
   Mr Quangle Wangle Quee!'

And besides, to the Crumpetty Tree
    Came the Stork, the Duck, and the Owl:
The Snail, and the Bumble-Bee,
    The Frog, and the Fimble Fowl;
(The Fimble Fowl, with a Corkscrew leg;)
And all of them said: 'We humbly beg,
We may build our homes on your lovely Hat:
Mr Quangle Wangle, grant us that!
    Mr Quangle Wangle Quee!'

And the Golden Grouse came there,
And the Pobble who has no toes,
And the small Olympian bear,
    And the Dong with a luminous nose.
And the Blue Baboon, who played the flute,
And the Orient Calf from the Land of Tute,
And the Attery Squash, and the Bisky Bat,
All came and built on the lovely Hat
    Of the Quangle Wangle Quee.

And the Quangle Wangle said
To himself on the Crumpetty Tree:
'When all these creatures move
    What a wonderful noise there'll be!'
And at night by the light of the Mulberry moon
They danced to the Flute of the Blue Baboon,
On the broad green leaves of the Crumpetty Tree,
And all were as happy as happy could be,
    With the Quangle Wangle Quee.

Edward Lear

The Listeners

'Is there anybody there?' said the Traveller,
  Knocking on the moonlit door;
And his horse in the silence champed the grasses
  Of the forest's ferny floor:
And a bird flew up out of the turret,
  Above the Traveller's head:
And he smote upon the door again a second time;
  'Is there anybody there?' he said.
But no one descended to the Traveller;
  No head from the leaf-fringed sill
Leaned over and looked into his grey eyes,
  Where he stood perplexed and still.
But only a host of phantom listeners
  That dwelt in the lone house then
Stood listening in the quiet of the moonlight
  To that voice from the world of men:
Stood thronging the faint moonbeams on the dark stair
  That goes down to the empty hall,

Hearkening in an air stirred and shaken
  By the lonely Traveller's call.
And he felt in his heart their strangeness,
  Their stillness answering his cry,
While his horse moved, cropping the dark turf,
  'Neath the starred and leafy sky;
For he suddenly smote on the door, even
  Louder, and lifted his head: –
'Tell them I came, and no one answered,
  That I kept my word,' he said.
Never the least stir made the listeners,
  Though every word he spake
Fell echoing through the shadowiness of the still house
  From the one man left awake:
Ay, they heard his foot upon the stirrup,
  And the sound of iron on stone,
And how the silence surged softly backward,
  When the plunging hoofs were gone.

Walter de la Mare

A Visit from St. Nicholas

'Twas the night before Christmas, when all through the house
Not a creature was stirring, not even a mouse;
The stockings were hung by the chimney with care,
In hopes that St. Nicholas soon would be there;
The children were nestled all snug in their beds;
While visions of sugar-plums danced in their heads;
And mamma in her 'kerchief, and I in my cap,
Had just settled our brains for a long winter's nap –
When out on the lawn there arose such a clatter,
I sprang from my bed to see what was the matter.
Away to the window I flew like a flash,
Tore open the shutters, and threw up the sash.
The moon, on the breast of the new-fallen snow,
Gave the luster of midday to objects below;
When, what to my wondering eyes should appear,
but a miniature sleigh and eight tiny reindeer,
With a little old driver, so lively and quick,
I knew in a moment it must be St. Nick.

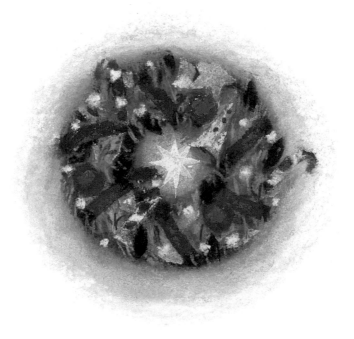

More rapid than eagles his coursers they came,
And he whistled, and shouted, and called them by name:
'Now *Dasher!* now, *Dancer!* now, *Prancer* and *Vixen!*
On, *Comet!* on, *Cupid!* on, *Donder* and *Blitzen!*
To the top of the porch! to the top of the wall!
Now dash away! dash away! dash away all!'
As dry leaves that before the wild hurricane fly,
When they meet with an obstacle, mount to the sky;
So up to the house-top the coursers they flew
With the sleigh full of toys, and St. Nicholas too.
And then, in a twinkling, I heard on the roof
The prancing and pawing of each little hoof –
As I drew in my head, and was turning around,
Down the chimney St. Nicholas came with a bound.
He was dressed all in fur, from his head to his foot,
And his clothes were all tarnished with ashes and soot;
A bundle of toys he had flung on his back,
And he looked like a pedlar just opening his pack.
His eyes – how they twinkled; his dimples, how merry!
His cheeks were like roses, his nose like a cherry!

His droll little mouth was drawn up like a bow,
And the beard of his chin was as white as the snow;
The stump of a pipe he held tight in his teeth,
And the smoke it encircled his head like a wreath;
He had a broad face and a little round belly
That shook, when he laughed, like a bowl full of jelly.
He was chubby and plump, a right jolly old elf,
And I laughed when I saw him, in spite of myself;
A wink of his eye and a twist of his head
Soon gave me to know I had nothing to dread;
He spoke not a word, but went straight to his work,
And filled all the stockings; then turned with a jerk,
And laying his finger aside of his nose,
And giving a nod, up the chimney he rose;
He sprang to his sleigh, to his team gave a whistle,
And away they all flew like the down of a thistle.
But I heard him exclaim, ere he drove out of sight,
'Happy Christmas to all, and to all a good night!'
                                    Clement Clarke Moore

Keep a Poem in Your Pocket

Keep a poem in your pocket
and a picture in your head
and you'll never feel lonely
at night when you're in bed.

The little poem will sing to you
the little picture bring to you
a dozen dreams to dance to you
at night when you're in bed.

So—
Keep a picture in your pocket
and a poem in your head
and you'll never feel lonely
at night when you're in bed.

Beatrice Schenk de Regniers

INDEX OF TITLES

INDEX OF FIRST LINES

INDEX OF AUTHORS

CREDITS AND PERMISSIONS

The editor and publisher are grateful for permission to include the following copyright material in this volume.

JOHN AGARD: 'Duppy Dan' from Black Poetry (Penguin, 1990) and 'First Morning' from Another Day on Your Foot and I Would Have Died (Macmillan Children's Books, 1997). Reprinted by permission of John Agard c/o Caroline Sheldon Literary Agency.

W. H. AUDEN: 'O What is that Sound' from Collected Shorter Poems 1927-1957 (Faber & Faber, 1966), © W. H. Auden, 1966. Reprinted by permission of Faber & Faber Ltd and Random House Inc.

HILAIRE BELLOC: 'The Frog' from The Complete Verse of Hilaire Belloc (Pimlico, 1991). Reprinted by permission of The Peters Fraser & Dunlop Group on behalf of The Estate of Hilaire Belloc.

LAURENCE BINYON: 'The Little Dancers' from The Nation's Favourite Poems of Childhood (BBC Consumer Publishing, 2000). Reprinted by permission of The Society of Authors on behalf of the Laurence Binyon Estate.

GERALD BULLETT: 'First Love' from Windows on a Vanished Time (Michael Joseph, 1955), © Gerald Bullett, 1955. Reprinted by permission of The Peters Fraser & Dunlop Group on behalf of The Estate of Gerald Bullett.

CHARLES CAUSLEY: 'I Had a Little Cat' from Selected Poems for Children (Macmillan, 1997), 'I Saw a Jolly Hunter' from Figgie Hobbin: Poems for Children (Macmillan, 1971), and 'Who?' from Collected Poems 1951-1992 (Macmillan, 1992). Reprinted by permission of David Higham Associates on behalf of the author.

WENDY COPE: 'Valentine' from Serious Concerns (Faber & Faber, 1992). Reprinted by permission of the publisher.

ANNE CORKETT: 'This I Know' from The Salamander's Laughter and other poems (Natural Heritage/Natural History, 1985), © 1985. Reprinted by permission of the author.

FRANCES CORNFORD: 'Dogs' from Collected Poems (Cresset Press, 1954). Reprinted by permission of The Random House Group.

E. E. CUMMINGS: 'maggie and milly and molly and may' from Complete Poems 1904-1962, edited by George J. Firmage (Norton, 1991), © 1991 by the Trustees for the E. E. Cummings Trust and George James Firmage. Reprinted by permission of W. W. Norton & Company.

ROALD DAHL: an extract from George's Marvellous Medicine (Jonathan Cape, 1981). Reprinted by permission of David Higham Associates on behalf of the Estate of Roald Dahl.

W. H. DAVIES: 'Leisure' from The Complete Poems of W. H. Davies (Jonathan Cape, 1963). Reprinted by permission of Dee & Griffin (Solicitors) on behalf of Mrs H. M. Davies Will Trust.

WALTER DE LA MARE: 'Silver' and 'The Listeners' from Selected Poems (Faber & Faber, 1973). Reprinted by permission of The Literary Trustees of Walter de la Mare and The Society of Authors as their representative.

BEATRICE SCHENK DE REGNIERS: 'Keep a Poem in Your Pocket' from Something Special (Harcourt Brace Jovanovich, 1958), © 1958 by Beatrice Schenk de Regniers. Reprinted by permission of Marian Reiner (Literary Agent).

EMILY DICKINSON: #101 ('Will there really be a "morning"') from The Poems of Emily Dickinson, edited by Thomas H. Johnson (Cambridge, Mass.: The Belknap Press of Harvard University Press), © 1951, 1955, 1979 by the President and Fellows of Harvard College. Reprinted by permission of the publishers and the Trustees of Amherst College.

JOHN DRINKWATER: 'Moonlit Apples' from Everyman's Book of Evergreen Verse, edited by David Herbert (Dent, 1993). Reprinted by permission of Samuel French Ltd on behalf of the Estate of John Drinkwater.

ELEANOR FARJEON: 'There Isn't Time!' and 'Waking Up' from Blackbird Has Spoken, edited by Anne Harvey (Macmillan Children's Books, 2000). Reprinted by permission of David Higham Associates.

MAX FATCHEN: 'Look Out!' from Songs for My Dog And Other People (Kestrel Books, 1980). Reprinted by permission of John Johnson (Authors' Agent) Ltd on behalf of the author.

RACHEL FIELD: 'Something Told the Wild Geese' from Poems (Macmillan Publishing Company, 1957). Reprinted by permission of Simon & Schuster Books for Young Readers, an imprint of Simon & Schuster Children's Publishing Division.

ROBERT FROST: 'The Road Not Taken' from The Poetry of Robert Frost, edited by Edward Connery Lathem (Henry Holt, 1969), copyright 1944 by Robert Frost, © 1916, 1969 by Henry Holt & Company. Reprinted by permission of Henry Holt & Company LLC and The Random House Group.

ROSE FYLEMAN: 'Singing-Time' from The Fairy Queen (George H. Doran Co., 1923). Reprinted by permission of The Society of Authors as the Literary Representative of the Estate of Rose Fyleman.

CHIEF DAN GEORGE: 'And my heart soars' from My Spirit Soars (Hancock House, 1989), © 1974 by Chief Dan George and Helmut Hirnschall.

KENNETH GRAHAME: 'Ducks' Ditty' from The Wind in the Willows (Methuen, 1908), © The University Chest, Oxford. Reprinted by permission of Curtis Brown Ltd., London.

DAVID GREYGOOSE: 'It's Only the Storm' from Language in Colour, edited by Moira Andrew (Belair, 1989).

SEAMUS HEANEY: 'The Railway Children' from New Selected Poems 1966-1987 (Faber & Faber, 1990). Reprinted by permission of the publisher.

EMILY HEARN: 'My Friend' from Hockey Cards & Hopscotch (Nelson Canada, 1980), © 1971. Reprinted by permission of Nelson Thomson Learning, a division of Thomson Learning.

CREDITS AND PERMISSIONS